D1125222

When I took my son and his friend down to the oval near our house, they found: a dead tree, a piece of tin, some bamboo and an old roof tile. The boys took a couple of sticks and began tapping – they'd made their own percussion orchestra! That afternoon I was telling Barbara about the interesting, spooky sounds the boys had made.

'Hmm,' she said thoughtfully, 'ghosts can make very spooky sounds. Imagine an old house where no one's lived for years, haunted by gruesome ghosts...'

Just then the boys blew into their hollow pieces of bamboo – 'whooo, whooo' – they went, sending shivers down my spine and Barbara running home with a truly spirited idea...

ANNA AND BARBARA FIENBERG

Anna and Barbara Fienberg write the Tashi stories together, making up all kinds of daredevil adventures and tricky characters for him to face. Lucky he's such a clever Tashi.

Kim Gamble is one of Australia's favourite illustrators for children. Together Kim and Anna have made such wonderful books as *The Magnificent Nose and Other Marvels*, *The Hottest Boy Who Ever Lived*, the *Tashi* series, the *Minton* picture books, *Joseph,* and a full colour picture book about their favourite adventurer, *There once was a boy called Tashi.*

For Stefano Pepe and James Tennant,
our splendid sources of inspiration.
Thank you!

First published in 2002
This edition first published in 2006

Allen & Unwin
83 Alexander St
Crows Nest NSW 2065
Australia
Phone: (61 2) 8425 0100
Fax: (61 2) 9906 2218
Email: info@allenandunwin.com
Web: www.allenandunwin.com

Cataloguing-in-Publication details are available
from the National Library of Australia
www.trove.nla.gov.au

ISBN 978 1 74114 953 1

Cover and series design by Sandra Nobes
Typeset in Sabon by Tou-Can Design
This book was printed in February 2012 at McPherson's Printing Group,
76 Nelson St, Maryborough, Victoria 3465, Australia.
www.mcphersonsprinting.com.au

10 9 8

www.tashibooks.com

Tashi

and the
HAUNTED
HOUSE

written by
Anna Fienberg
and
Barbara Fienberg

•

illustrated by
Kim Gamble

ALLEN&UNWIN

'Well, look who's here!' cried Uncle Joe,
as he spied Tashi strolling up the garden
path. He leapt from his chair and sprinted
across the lawn.

'I was just thinking about you, my boy!
There's someone *special* I want you to meet.'
Uncle Joe's eyes were dancing and he kept
fidgeting in his pockets and sucking at his
moustache while he shot quick, shy glances
around the garden.

5

The rest of the family were busy digging
and planting for Spring. Tashi saw a new
herb patch near the steps and Jack was
potting a tomato plant. Suddenly, a dark-
haired lady stepped out from behind the
box hedge.

'Primrose! There you are!' Joe cried
proudly.

Primrose smiled and put out her hand
for Tashi to shake.

Uncle Joe looked from one to the other, beaming. 'I met Primrose up north, you see, when I was camping by a river *jumping* with barramundi.'

'Oh, so that's where you went after you walked through the kitchen wall?' Tashi asked with interest.

'Yes, yes, and I told dear Primrose all about your ghostly adventures, Tashi, as she and I fished by the river in the moonlight and fell hopelessly in love. Do you know, Primrose is not only the best angler I've met in my time but she's also an amazing musician. A percussionist!'

'I just tap on things,' Primrose said mildly. She picked up a teaspoon lying on the table and tapped lightly on the glasses and jugs, making a tinkling little tune.

'What I like best, though,' Primrose said confidingly to Tashi, 'is to make sounds with things from the natural world. I'm always searching for different, curious things to tap.'

Just then Jack came over, his hands black with dirt. 'Do you know, Tashi, Primrose can make scary, ghostly noises, just with bottles and wood and things? If you close your eyes and listen, you'd swear a million ghosts were breathing down your neck!'

Tashi nodded as Mum began pouring lemonade for everyone.

'You remind me of my cousin, Lotus Blossom,' Tashi said to Primrose.

'What, the one who keeps disappearing?' Joe asked in alarm.

'Yes,' said Tashi. 'But not because of that. No, once Lotus Blossom and I were in a situation of terrible danger and we needed to summon up the sound of ghostly voices. She did it very well.'

'Ghosts, eh Tashi?' put in Dad, as he peeled off his gardening gloves. He nudged Joe happily.

'So, tell us about Lotus Blossom,' said
Primrose. 'Was she a percussionist like me?'

'No,' grinned Tashi. 'She was a pest. But
she did have some good ideas. Especially
when it came to the haunted house.'

Everyone watched as Tashi took a sip
of lemonade.

'Go on,' urged Mum.

'Well, it was like this. Ever since I can
remember, the ghost house has been there,

crouching in the gloomiest part of the forest. No one from our village had set foot in that place, ever. Well, not for thirty years, anyway. Not since something dreadful happened to the old couple who used to live there. We children could never find out exactly *what* happened. The grown-ups would look frightened when we asked and say, "We don't want to talk about it."'

Jack snorted. 'That'd be right.'

'Sometimes we'd scare ourselves sick by running past the house or dare each other to go right up the path. So far only Ah Chu and I had actually dared to creep up and knock on the door.

'Then one winter's evening, Ah Chu's father caught up with us on the way home. He'd been in the forest burning charcoal and his hands were black with soot. They looked a bit like yours, Jack! But I still remember how they trembled when he shook my shoulder.

'Don't go near the ghost house,' he warned. 'I've just seen a light flickering in the window. Who knows *what* is prowling around in there!'

'Wah! He hurried on his way and we went on making our dam in the creek. Neither of us said a word, but you can be sure we were both thinking about the ghost house, and the strange light burning there. We knew that the next day we would just have to go and see for ourselves.

'Darkness comes early in those winter afternoons so we hurried through the forest, our hearts thumping at every bird calling, or branch snapping.'

Cra-ack! Primrose broke a stick over her knee and Dad nearly fell off his chair.

'Sorry,' she whispered. 'I was just adding sound effects.'

'Well, Lotus Blossom came with us that afternoon because she hates to miss out on anything and, besides, she said she would tell Ah Chu's father if we didn't let her come. Off she went running as fast as she could through the trees, far ahead of us, until we lost sight of her. But when we drew near the house, wasn't she leaning against a tree, panting, with a stitch in her side?

'I couldn't help laughing, but then Ah Chu said he had to stop too, because he had a pebble in his shoe and a sore foot. So I had to go up the path alone.

'I crept along slowly, over patches of damp green moss and through vines as thick as your fist. The house rose up before me, dark and full of shadows – it was like an animal in its lair, half hidden by the webbed shade of the trees.

'The latch lifted stiffly in my clammy hand and the door creaked open. "Come *on*!" I called over my shoulder and waited while Ah Chu and Lotus Blossom pushed each other up the path.

'I went first. It was black as a bat's cave inside, and smelled of mould. The further in we crept, the colder it grew. It was like walking into a grave. Something sticky and soft brushed against my face – *ugh!* – spiderwebs! When my eyes grew used to the dark I saw dust hanging in long strands from the rafters like ghostly grey ribbons.

'Then Lotus Blossom yelped suddenly as her foot went through a rotten floorboard. Wah! She nearly fell through the hole!

'"I thought something grabbed my ankle," she whispered.

'We clung together, listening to the silence. Even our breathing was loud. And then came the sound of a careful footstep from the room above our head. Ah Chu moaned.

'I stepped forward. "Is anybody there?" I called.

'We heard a creak and a flurry of steps and then *crash*! A great beam that had been holding up the ceiling came hurtling down, landing in a huge cloud of dust just millimetres from my nose.

'We all reached the door at once, so for a moment no one could get out. Ah Chu is quite plump and almost filled the doorway by himself but he and Lotus Blossom finally pushed through and were down the path like pellets out of a peashooter.

'I was about to follow, I can tell you – '

'Quick, quick, didn't you get out of there?' cried Jack.

'Well, I looked back, just for a second, and there, sprawled among the rubble of the fallen ceiling was a young woman. She lifted her head and groaned, so I raced back to her.

'"Are you hurt? Have you broken something?"

'She tried to stand up. "My ankle aches terribly," she whispered. "Oh, I knew the floor was rotten but I was so frightened. I thought you were someone sent by my cousin to take me back." She looked at me closely. "You're not, are you?"

'"No, I'm Tashi. I don't even know your cousin. Why are you so scared of him?"

'"When my mother and father died, my cousin Bu Li moved in. I always hated him – he's so much older than me and strong as an ox. He kept me locked in the house from morning till night, dyeing his silk. "You'll stay here and be my slave," he bellowed at me everyday, "until you tell me where you've hidden that emerald ring your mother left you." But I *wouldn't*! She told me before she died that I could use it to start a new life, and that is what I'm going to do."

'Ning Jing, for that was her name, pulled out a little bag hanging on a string around her neck. I looked at the ring respectfully. It was the first emerald I'd ever seen; it was green like the moss outside, green like a cat's eyes in the dark.

'I noticed that Ning Jing was rubbing her ankle, so I said, "If your leg is hurting, why don't you stay here tonight and rest it?"

'Ning Jing nodded. "But I would need some food, Tashi. I have only this one fish cake left."

'"Tomorrow, straight after school, I'll bring you some more food from home. And then you can go on your way to the city."

'I had gone down the path only a little
way when Ah Chu and Lotus Blossom
popped out of some bushes to join me. We
stopped and sat for a while in the gathering
dusk as they peppered me with questions.
I told them all about Ning Jing and her
horrible cousin, and the emerald winking
like a cat's eye.

'"Thank the Gods of Long Life," sighed
Lotus Blossom. "I'm so glad that the ghost
was instead a Ning Jing!"

'They both promised that they would
come with me the next day with the food.

24

'Never was a day so long. As soon as school was over we raced home to collect the food. Ah Chu, who always took a great interest in eating, raided his mother's kitchen so well that he took an age to arrive, laden down with heavy baskets. And that is why, of course, he needed to sit down for a little rest on the way to the house while we went on ahead. And that's how he came to hear three men blundering about in the forest. He pricked up his ears like a fox when he heard the name Ning Jing.

'"Demon of a woman!" hissed the man with the long thin beard. "That Ning Jing – her mother was just like her. Stubborn as a mule, tricky as a weasel. Now which way did she go?"

'"There's no track here, no sign of her at all."

'"Well if you'd been keeping your eyes peeled instead of picking berries and stuffing yourself, we wouldn't have lost her!"

'When Ah Chu had heard enough, he stood up quietly and trickled off through the trees.

'Bursting into the ghost house, he cried, "Three men are looking for Ning Jing in the forest."

'"Does one man have a long straggly beard?" asked Ning Jing. When Ah Chu told her, she buried her face in her hands. "I can't fight my cousin any more," she murmured through her fingers. "Oh what will I do, Tashi?"

'She looked straight at me then, and so did the others. I was just beginning to feel a little bit annoyed about people always asking me that question, when I had an idea.

'"Don't worry," I said to Ning Jing.
"I've just thought of a plan. Ah Chu, you
hurry back to where you saw the men.
Tell them you've seen a young woman –
a stranger in the forest – and that she's
staying the night in an old empty house
close by. Don't forget to mention that the
house is haunted, and something dreadful
once happened there."

'Then I told Lotus Blossom that her job
was to follow Ah Chu, but to stay hidden
from the men. "You've got to make sure
that they're all thinking about ghosts by the
time they reach this house."

'"How?" she asked.'

'By making ghostly noises!' cried Primrose suddenly. And she blew into the empty lemonade bottle on the garden table, making a low wheezy moan.

'That's it, my clever one!' cried Uncle Joe, squeezing her arm.

'You've got it!' agreed Tashi. 'I told Lotus Blossom I didn't know quite how she'd do it, but I knew she'd think of something.

'Well, Ah Chu quickly found the men in the forest as they were still standing there arguing.

'"Take us to the girl then, young fellow," said Cousin Bu Li, "and you'll have a little something for your trouble." Turning to his men he laughed, "And he'll get a fist in the belly if he doesn't!"

'"Ooh, sir, I don't know if I can, sir," shuddered Ah Chu, making his hands tremble. "That old house is haunted, ever since two people were murdered there... hung by their necks from the rafters!"

'"Haunted eh?" cousin Bu Li crowed. "A fine place she's chosen to hide. Why, she'll be glad to see us!"

'But Ah Chu noticed how pale he'd suddenly become.

'As they moved through the forest, the men grew quiet and jumpy. Suddenly they heard a low wailing and whistling like a whipping autumn wind. They stopped and peered around. But not a leaf moved in the stillness. Cousin Bu Li shivered. "Just a bird," he muttered, and moved on.

'A minute passed and now there came thin whooshing sounds like a hundred Samurai swords swiping at the air. Then a tremendous rattling noise of thunder made the men hold their hands to their ears, but the sky above them was clear and still as a piece of blue silk. A blood-curdling shriek – like a man having his throat cut from ear to ear – rushed the men through the forest, clutching onto each other's coats as they went.

'When they arrived at the path leading to the house, Cousin Bu Li needed all his promises of gold to urge the men on.

'"Ning Jing!" he shouted. "Come out at once or you'll be sorry for the rest of your short and miserable life!"

'There was no sound.

'The men edged into the house. They tasted the damp and the dust. They peered through the dark and the cobwebs. Then a deep shuddery wailing started and the men looked up to see a gaping black hole in the ceiling. The wail poured out of the darkness, filling the room like a river rushing into the sea.

'The two men turned and fled. Only cousin Bu Li stood his ground. Then the hairs on his neck stiffened.

'A light appeared, shining up into the
hole in the ceiling. It lit up a ghastly sight:
Ning Jing's headless body (he knew it was
Ning Jing because that was her dress with
the blue peacock on the front) and it was
swinging from an iron hook. A sob drew
his horrified gaze to an old chest in the
corner. Resting on the top of the chest was
... her head. The eyes in the head wept and

the mouth sobbed, "Oh, cousin, why did you drive me to my death?"

'Cousin Bu Li screamed and raced for the door. He bolted out of the house and ran so fast through the forest that he caught up with his men, passed them in a flash and left them far behind. He never went near that forest again for as long as he lived.

'Meanwhile, I wriggled out of Ning Jing's dress. You see, she was taller than me so the collar of her dress had covered my head. Ah Chu and Lotus Blossom, who had arrived back a few minutes before, helped me down and Ning Jing came out from behind the chest. She and her head skipped over to join us.

'"Oh, Tashi, that was wonderful. I'll never forget Cousin Bu Li's face when he looked up and saw – what he thought he saw!"

'Lotus Blossom was really cross. She said it was all very well for us, but she and Ah Chu hadn't heard about the plan and they'd had a nasty shock when they saw that swinging body and talking head. She shivered, saying the next time I had a clever idea I needn't bother to invite her along.

'"Well, who invited *you*?" I said, and she gave me a good pinch on the arm!

'Later, as we were enjoying a little snack of Ah Chu's food, I said to Ning Jing, "It was strange that you happened to be in the haunted house the very day we came."

'"Not so strange," said Ning Jing. "This house once belonged to my grandparents."

'"It did?" we cried. "What happened to them?"

'"What? What?"

'Ning Jing looked thoughtful. "I think that is something you should ask your parents."

Tashi sat back in his chair and grinned at Jack. 'And that was all we were ever able to find out.'

Jack said disgustedly, 'All grown-ups are the same, even the young ones. They never tell you anything.'

'Some do. Percussionists do,' argued Primrose. 'For example, I could tell you what Lotus Blossom used to make that whistling wind sound, the whipping Samuari swords, or the rattle like thunder.'

'Lotus Blossom probably told Tashi everything already,' protested Jack.

Tashi leaned forward and tapped his glass. 'No, she didn't, Jack. We had quite an argument, actually. I suppose she was still mad with me about the fright she got.' Tashi grinned into his lemonade. 'So, Primrose, how did she do it?'

'Well, come down into the garden and I'll show you. Now, let's see, what'll we need? Some small branches for whipping swords, I think, and pebbles to turn in a basin...'

But Jack and Tashi had already leapt up and dashed off across the lawn. Blood-curdling shrieks were heard as they disappeared amongst the trees.

THE BIG RACE

Jack burst into the kitchen on Monday
afternoon. 'Guess what happened at school
today!'

'What?' cried Mum and Uncle Joe and
Primrose, who stopped playing the conga
drums to listen.

'Our class was in the assembly hall and we were doing a stomping dance when suddenly the stage floor fell in beneath us – '

'Batter the barramundi, was anyone hurt?' asked Uncle Joe.

'No,' replied Jack. 'Mrs Fitzpatrick leapt across the stage and saved Angus Figment who was right on the edge of this great ginormous hole. All the teachers gathered around and asked why wasn't there *ever* enough money for public schools and now they'd have to come up with *another* amazing idea for fund-raising to fix the floor, when Tashi stepped in – '

'Ho ho!' cried Dad, who'd just come in the door.

'Yes, and Tashi said, really quietly, you know how he is, that back in the old country he'd raised enough money to build a whole new school! When all the teachers asked "How?" Tashi said, "Well, it was like this – "'

Suddenly the kitchen was filled with a drum roll from the congas.

'Thank you, Primrose,' Mum said, holding her head. 'Perhaps we can leave that for the end of the story, dear.'

'Yes, let's,' agreed Primrose enthusiastically, 'or better, what about one super duper roll for the climax, and a soft, furry one for the finish?'

Mum nodded weakly. 'So, how did he do it, Jack?'

'Well, Tashi said everybody had known for ages that something would have to be done about their village school-house. The walls were all wrinkled and powdery with dry rot. Sometimes, the children could hear rustling sounds of white ants chewing at the wood.

'But it was an awful shock when suddenly one morning – luckily while everyone was outside – the large roof beam cracked and sagged. Just a minute later the whole building slowly collapsed, and the walls quietly fell in like buckling knees.'

'BOOF! BANG! BOOM!' went the drums.

'That's not the climax!' Mum protested. 'And didn't Jack say *quietly*?'

'Sorry,' grinned Primrose. 'I couldn't resist. That was an exclamation mark.'

'Well, anyway,' Jack went on, 'teacher Pang and the children stood open-mouthed at the sight of their school-house turned in one moment into a pile of dust and rubble.

'"What luck!" cried Ah Chu (who hated spelling tests). "No more school! Who's coming fishing?"

'"Not me," said Tashi. "Fishing is one thing, holidays are fun, but just think, to have no school at all, ever! It would be so boring."

'A meeting was called in the village to try to find a way of building a new school. A few people brought along some timber and roof tiles and put them in the middle of the square, but there was not nearly enough. No one had any money to spare, as usual.

'And then, two strangers wandered into the square. They were a mysterious-looking pair. Their clothes didn't quite fit and although their large hats hid most of their faces, Tashi thought he saw a pair of yellow tusks as one smiled. And there, as one stranger turned to point Tashi out to the other, Tashi saw a a tail poking out from under his coat! *Demons!*'

'Oh, *those* thick-headed thugs!' cried
Dad. 'Remember when they poured spiders
and snakes onto Tashi and he tricked them,
jumping into that old Dragon's Blood tree?'

'That's right,' said Jack. 'And that's why
Tashi was especially nervous now. Because
demons are always dangerous, but angry
demons with revenge in their hearts are
diabolical. And now what on earth were
they doing in his village square?

'The demons stood still as stones,
listening to all the talk and wild
suggestions. But finally one of them
boomed over all the voices.

"'No, no, what you must do is give us a race around the village! We'll race one of these children." He pointed a claw-finger at Tashi. "This little dillblot here, for instance. If he wins, we'll give you all the bricks and timber for a new school."

"'And if he loses?'"

"'If he loses, he'll be ours to do with as we will." And behind his hand he gave a laugh that cracked with demon spite.

'Oh *NO!*" cried the villagers and Tashi's family. Especially Tashi's family.

'But the Baron pushed through the crowd. "I think that's an excellent idea. Who would like to wager that Tashi wins?"

'The villagers were so eager to show their faith in Tashi that they all put their hands up before they realised they had been tricked into agreeing.

'"That's settled then," the Baron smiled nastily. The demons poked each other in the ribs and sniggered.

'*He's* the dillblot!' exploded Dad. 'That Baron could buy ten new school-houses for the village and not even dent his mountain of money. But would he? Never!'

'"First I'll go home and get my running shoes," Tashi told the villagers. "I'll be back here in one hour," he called over his shoulder.

'"Yes, so will we," hissed the demons and Tashi spied fat drops of drool sliding out from beneath their tusks.

'"Now where are they off to?" Tashi wondered as the family hurried home with him, begging him not to take part in the race.

'"Don't worry," Tashi comforted his mother. "I'll be quite safe with these on." And he pulled his magic dancing shoes out of the playbox in his room. "In just a few seconds I can leap across fields and forests with these."

'While he was putting on his shoes, he told the family that they were right to be suspicious about the strangers; they were the two demons who had tortured him with spiders and snakes once before. The family was horrified.

'"I thought there was something odd when they called you a dillblot," said Tashi's father. "What does that mean? I said to myself. Now I know – *demons* eh? They're famous for their poor vocabulary.

'Now Tashi, my boy, if you must do this, please test your shoes one last time to be sure that the magic is still working."

'Tashi agreed, and when they returned to the square all the villagers were waiting.

'The Wicked Baron raised his silk handkerchief. "Let the race begin!"

'The demons bared their tusks and their terrible eyes spun and blazed but at the

word "GO!" they shot off towards the forest. Tashi had never seen anyone run so fast.

'He waited until he felt his feet tingle
and then he was away. In two minutes
he had flashed past the astonished demons.
He'd just reached the half-way mark when,
as his foot touched the ground for the next
step, a loop of tough vine closed around it
and he was jerked upside down – he found
himself swinging from a tall tree. Hadn't
he stepped right into a Tashi-trap the
demons had prepared for him? *Wah!*

'In the distance he could see the demons coming nearer. He struggled and rocked himself in anguish. He knew what they would do to him once they found him dangling helplessly from a tree. He jerked and twisted but the vine held him fast.

'And then he noticed that he *was* swinging a little. He arched his back and drew up his knees. His swings grew wider and higher. Just a little more and he was able to grab at a branch of a tree and pull himself up.

'There were crashing sounds down in the bushes below and two hot and dripping demons went panting past. Tashi sat astride the branch and slipped the vine over his ankle. Then he scrambled down to the ground and set off again.

'He was just catching up with the
demons when he noticed that a mist was
rolling in through the trees. In an instant
it had thickened so much that the demons
ahead disappeared from sight. Tashi crept
on slowly, feeling his way, bumping into
trees. The fog was cold like a rain cloud,
and tasted stale and wet on his lips. He
kept blinking against the grey light but it
was as if a bandage had been pulled tight
over his eyes. He jumped when he heard
demon voices right beside him.

'"I can't believe you let the misty stuff out of the bottle in *front* of us instead of behind us! How did you reckon we'd find our way through this fog-thing?" shouted the first demon.

'"I didn't think," whined the second. "Couldn't you get it back in again?"

'"You can't put the fog-thing back into a bottle once it's out, you dillblot. Don't you know anything? At least Tashi won't be able to see either. We'll just have to sit here until it blows away. *Dill*blot."

'Tashi moved on carefully until his outstretched hands met a fence. He followed the fence around until he came to a familiar gatepost. "I know this gate!" he thought joyfully. "It belongs to Granny White Eyes."

'Granny White Eyes was so called because she could not see. Tashi and the other children of the village loved going to her house because she always had an interesting story to tell. Her brother had been a sailor and she'd accompanied him on many trips to exotic parts of the world.

'Tashi crawled up the garden path and knocked on the door. Lotus Blossom opened it.

'"Hello, Tashi. Oh, Granny White Eyes," she called into the darkness behind her, "it's Tashi come to see you!"

'An old woman came slowly to the door. "Tashi! Come in, what a lovely surprise. I wasn't expecting you today."

'"Well, this isn't exactly a visit," said Tashi. "It's like this," and he told her about the school-house and the demons and the race. "So," he finished, "I was wondering if you could lead me back to the village, Granny White Eyes."

"Of course I can," she laughed. "Mist or no mist, it makes no difference to me. I know every twist and turn in the path as well as my own kitchen. Come on."

'Tashi held on tight to her coat and they set off at a brisk pace through the blinding mist. Just before they reached the village, the fog cleared and Tashi stopped.

'"I can see now. Granny White Eyes, would you like to run like the wind with me on my magic shoes?"

'Her face creased into a wide smile. "Tashi, I would."

'Tashi knelt down and she climbed onto his shoulders. Granny screamed with delight as they sped over the ground.

'"Oh Tashi, I never thought I would fly through the air like this. It's wonderful."

'And didn't the village cheer as they zipped into the square? The people crowded around to hear what happened, nudging each other, trying to get close to Tashi. All except the Baron, of course. He went home.

'A bedraggled pair of demons finally found their way back to the village. They cursed and spat and "dillblotted" everywhere, but by late afternoon they had unloaded a cartful of bricks and tiles in the village square.

'And that is why the new school-house has Tashi's name over the door, and why sometimes, on cold Monday mornings, (especially when there's a spelling test) his friend Ah Chu mutters, "What a clever Tashi!"

Mum sighed happily, then jumped as if she'd been shot.

'BOOF! BANG! BOOM!' went the drums.

'You were a bit late weren't you, Primrose?' said Mum crossly.

'A little,' admitted Primrose. 'I got caught up in the story and forgot.'

'Well, I haven't forgotten about that stage floor at your school, Jack,' said Dad, shaking his head. 'Has Tashi spotted any helpful demons in this suburb?'

'Not yet,' said Jack. 'But he's keeping his eye out.'